SHADOW

REFLECTION

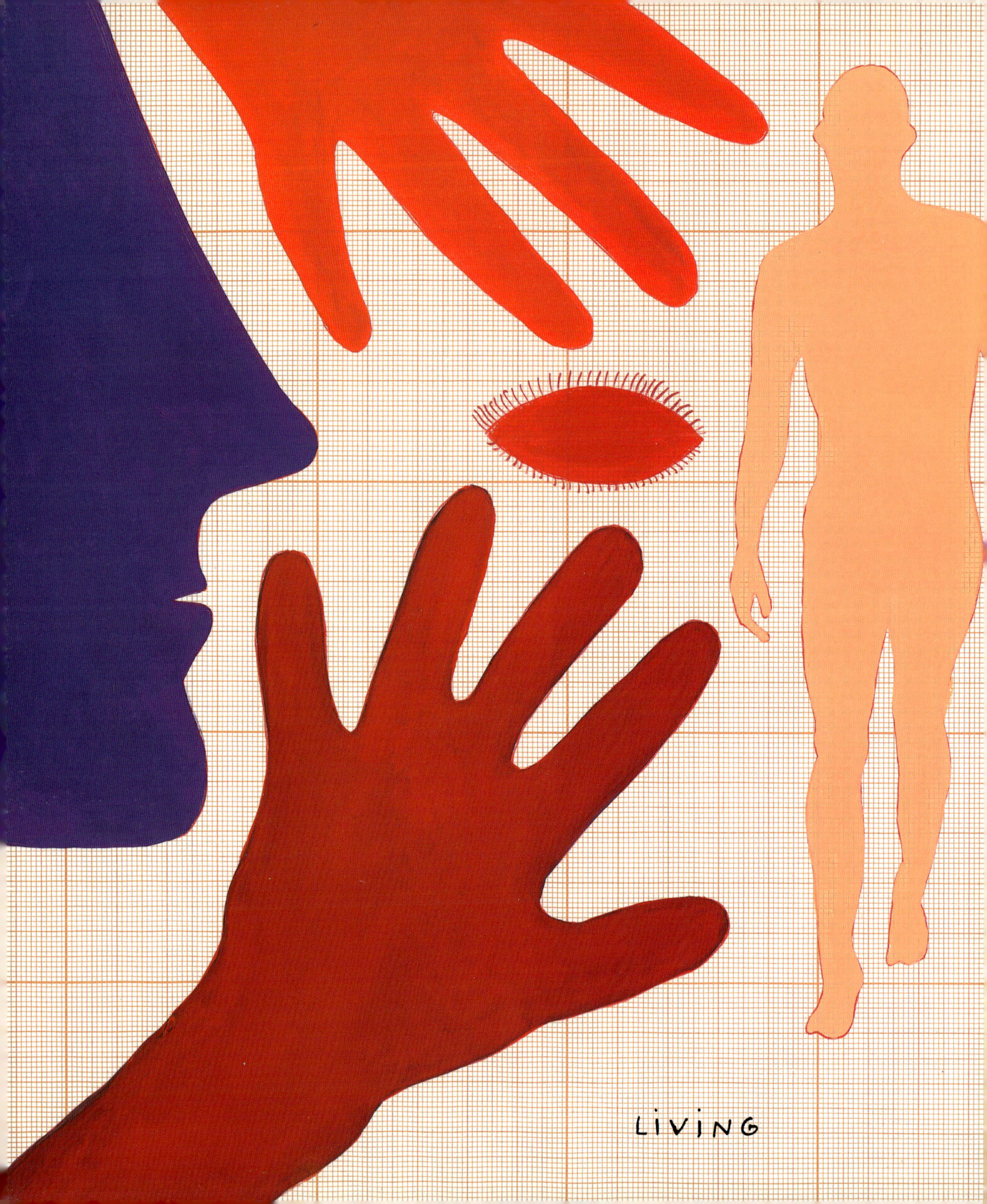

LIViNG

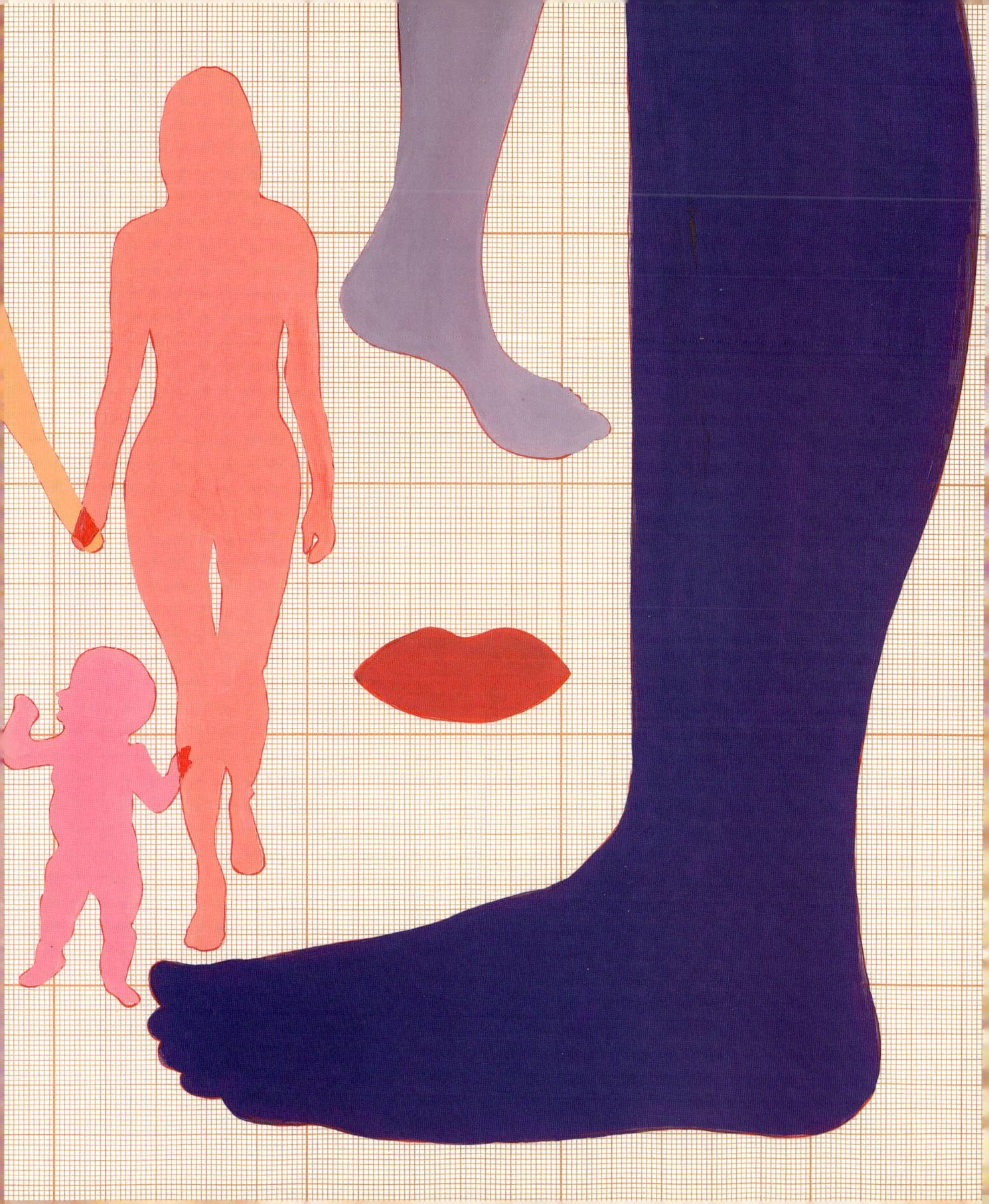

MOVING

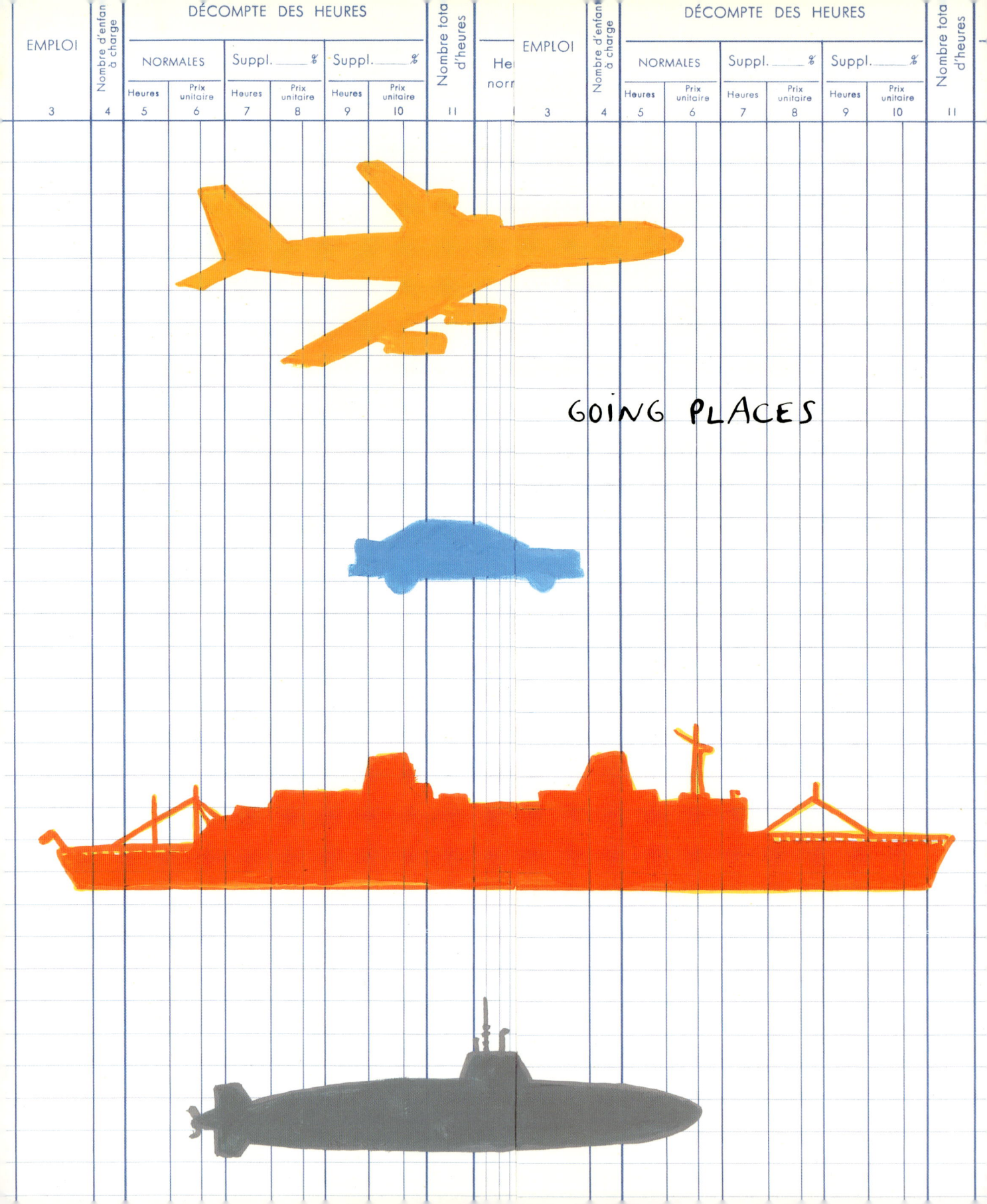

SIGHTSEEING

THE EARTH

THE UNIVERSE

ONE ANIMAL

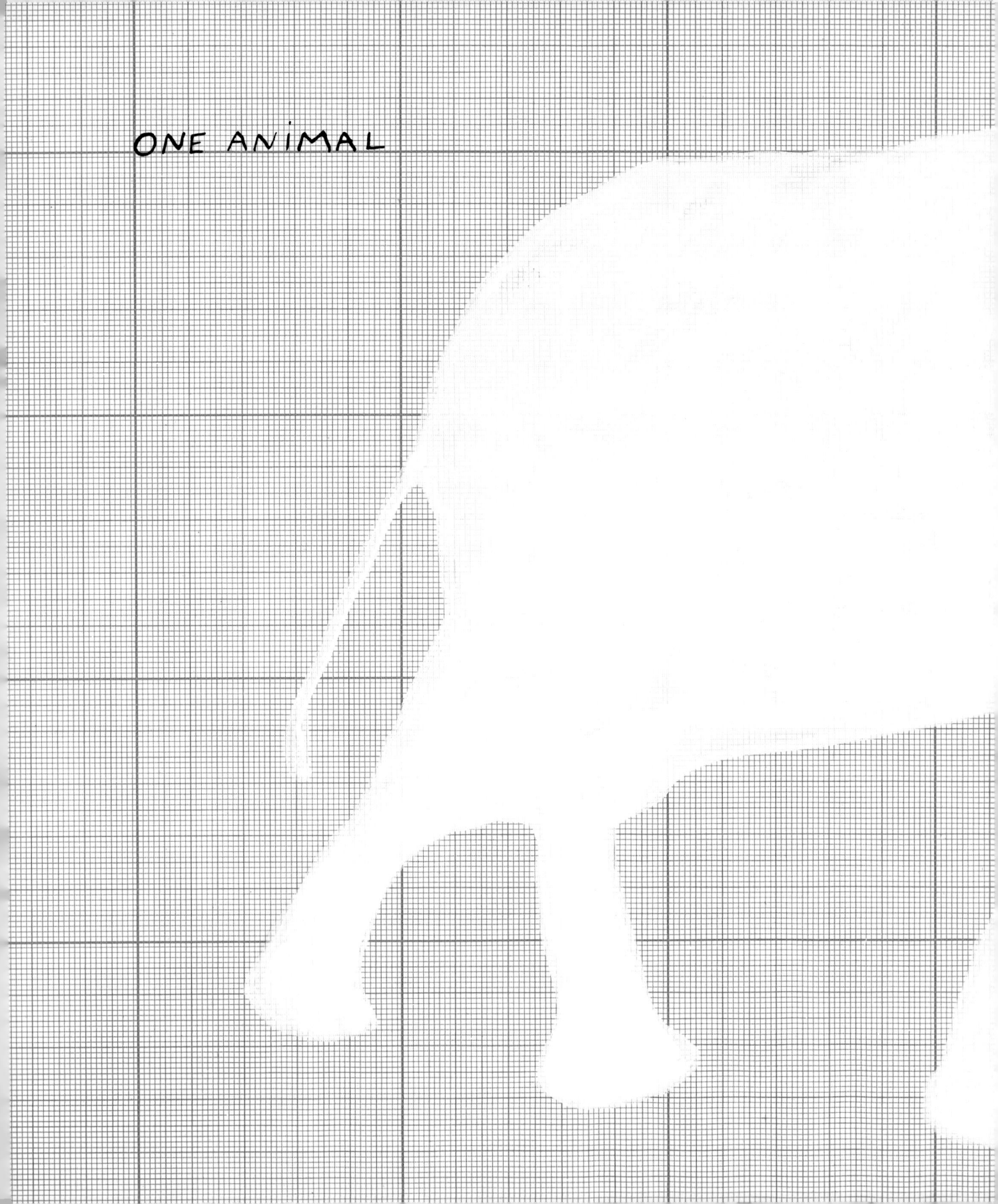

LOTS OF ANIMALS

LONG AGO

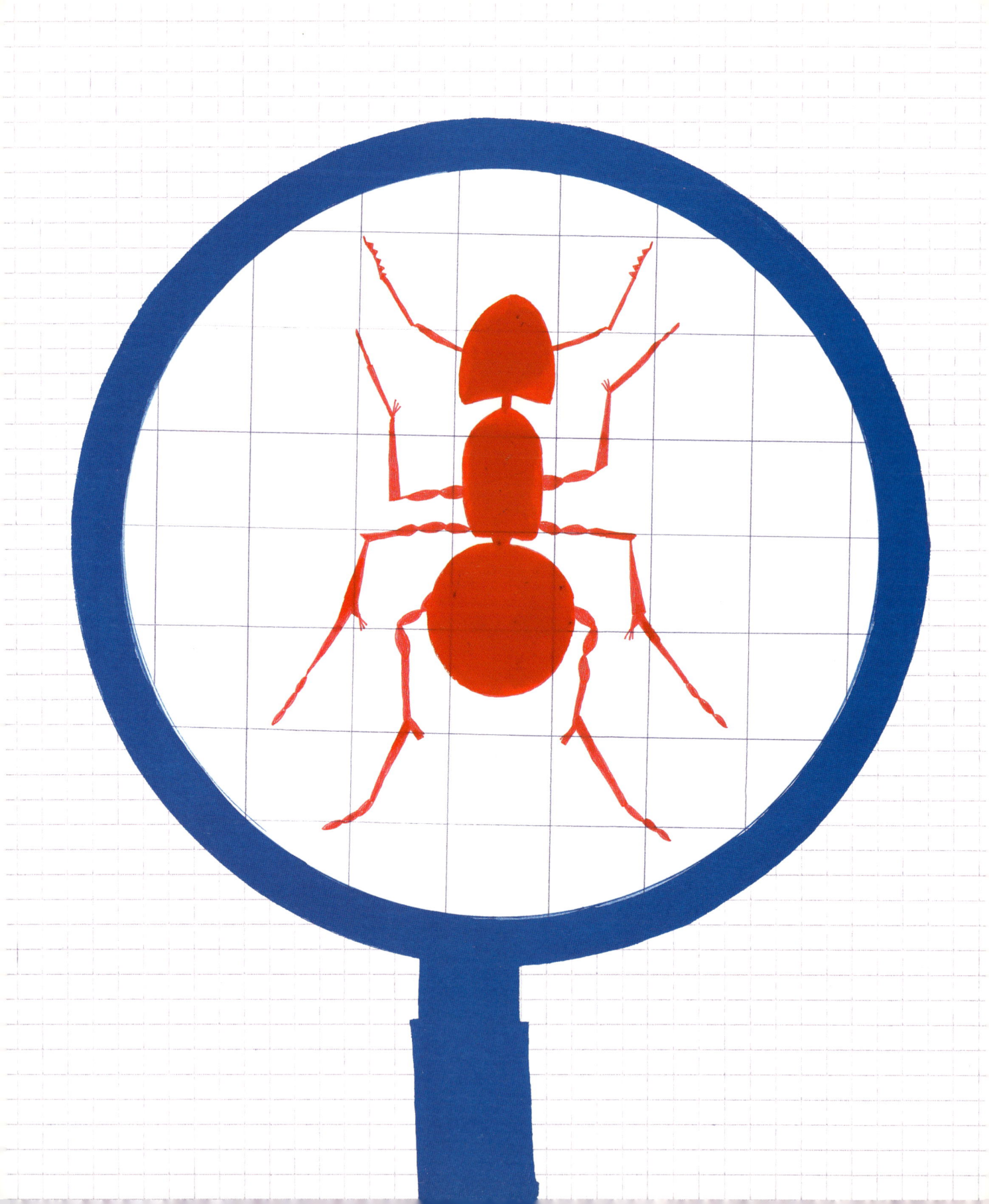

BUGS

IN THE SEA

ON THE ROAD

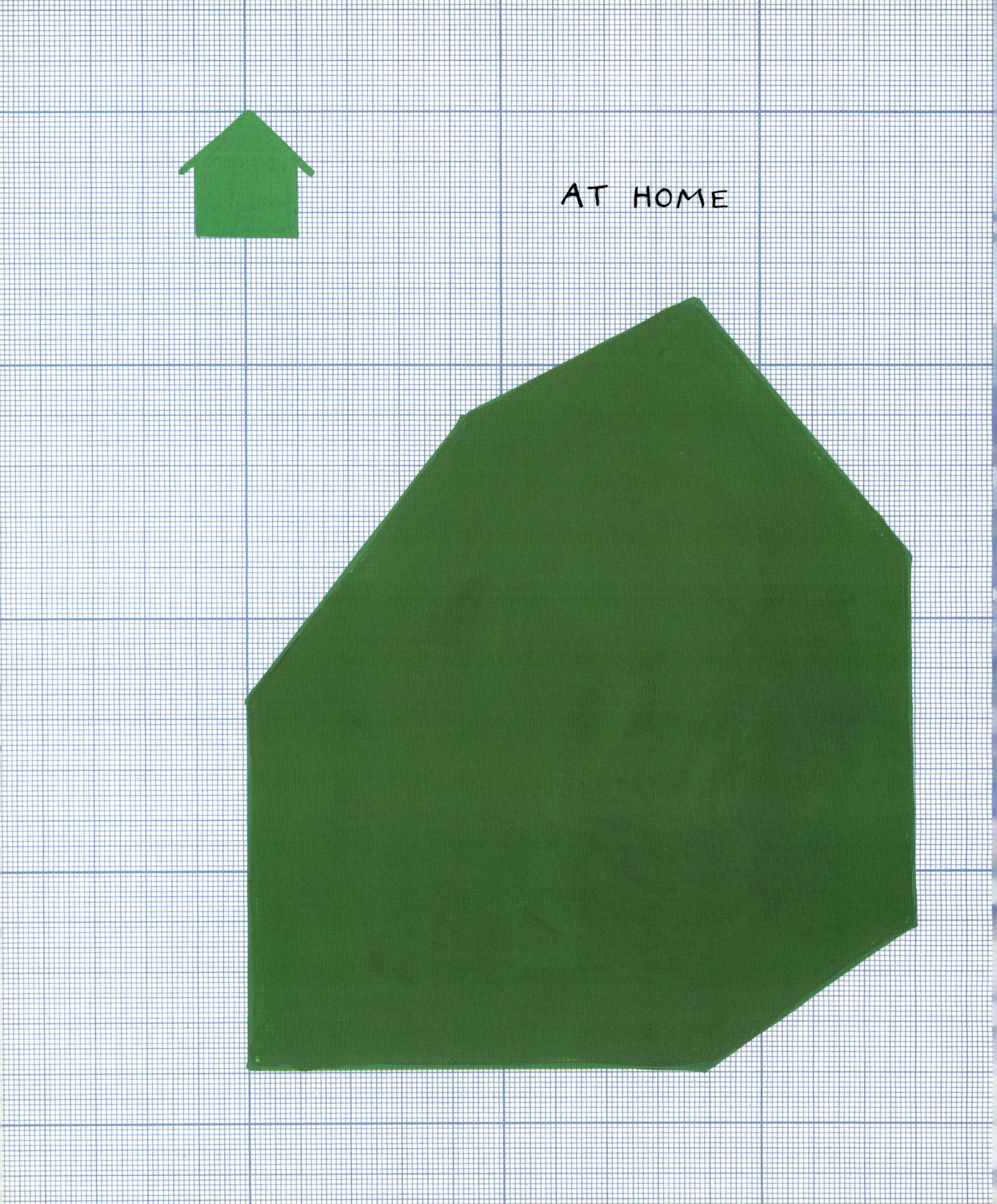

AT HOME

OPEN THE DOOR

COME INSIDE!

BATHROOM

BEDROOM

KITCHEN

EAT

HELP YOURSELF!

RED SHOES

GREEN BOOTS

SHOPPING

TOOLS

IN THE GARDEN

SEASONS

GiViNG

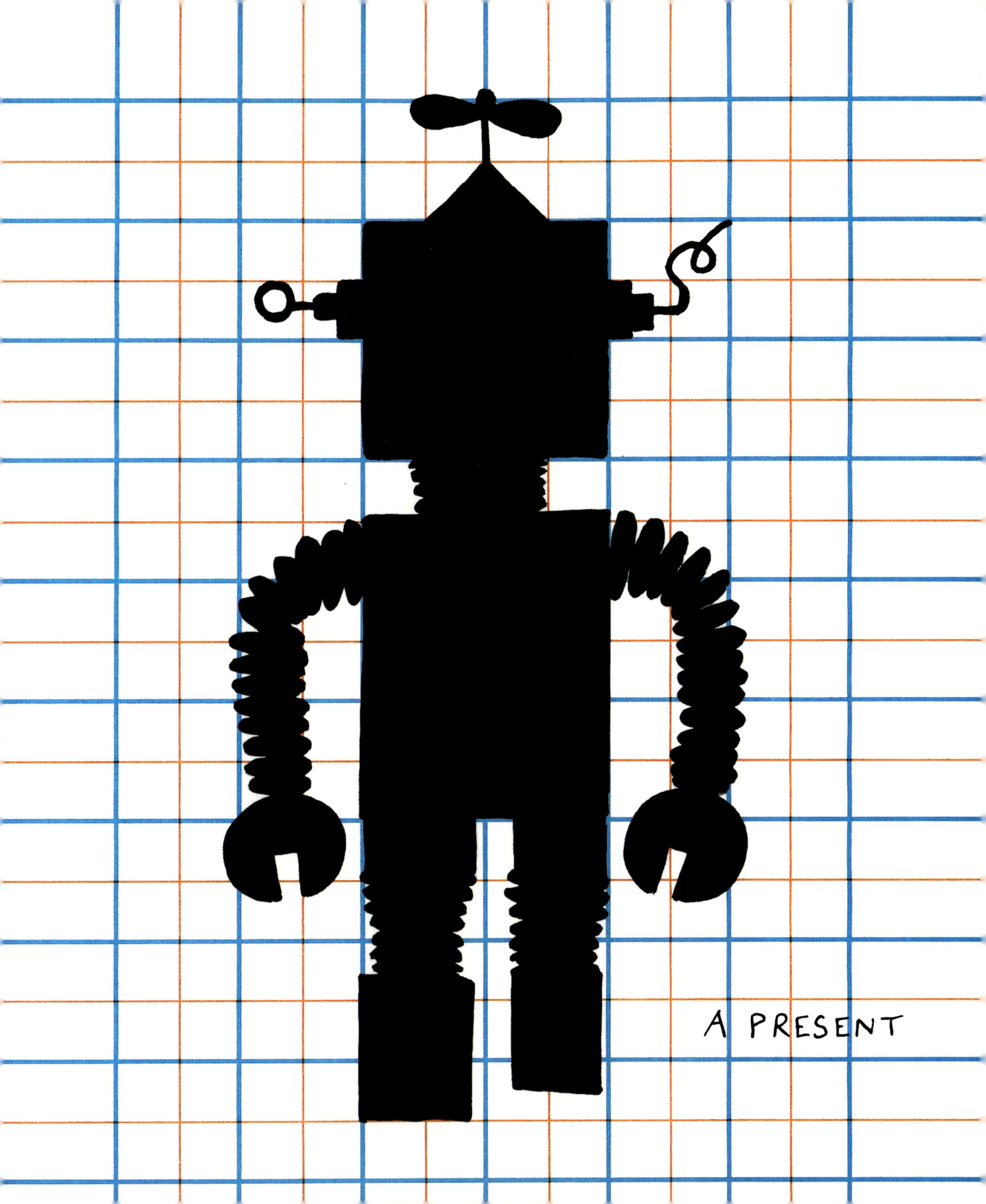

A PRESENT

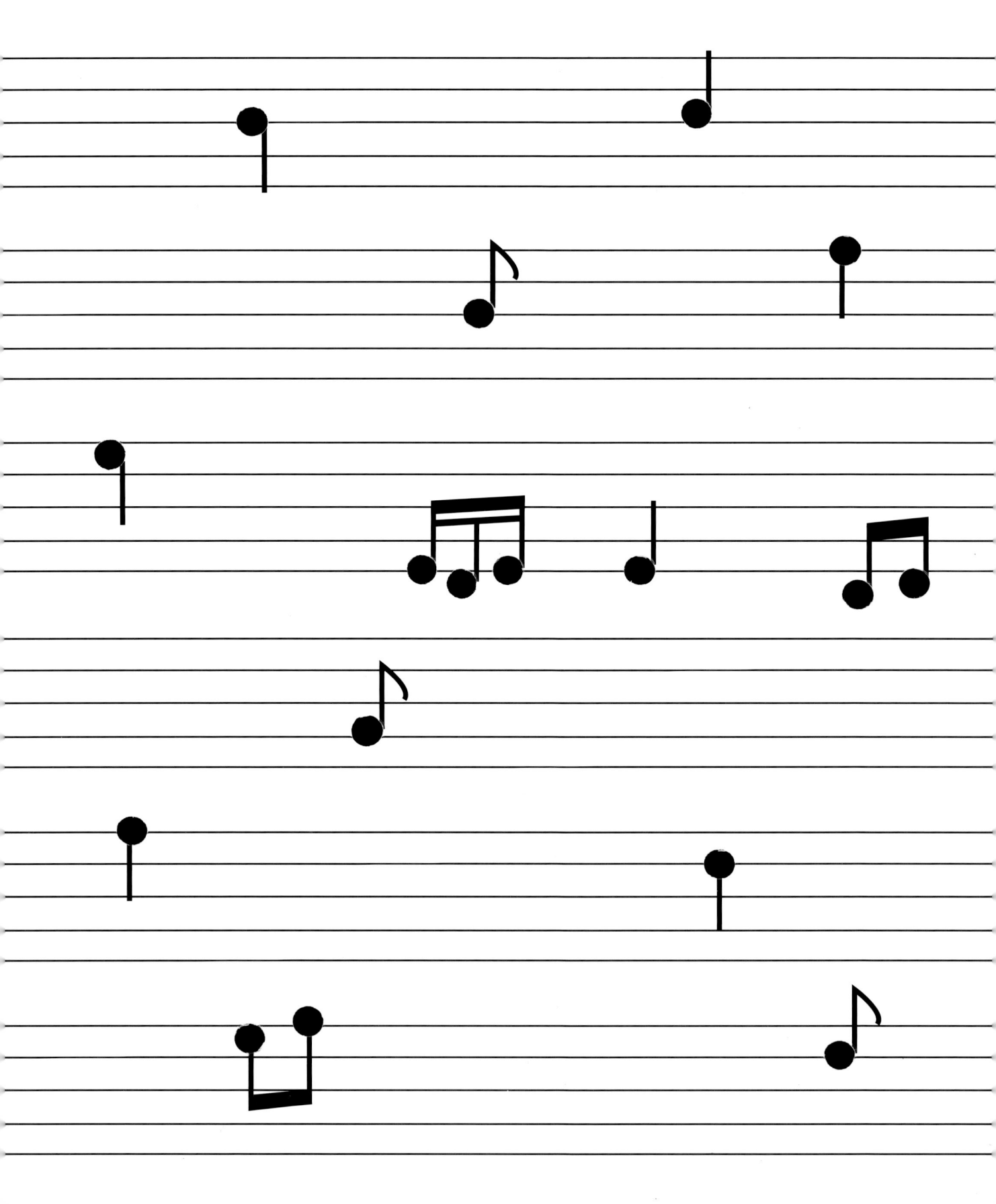

PAINTINGS

CUT APART

STICK TOGETHER

DREAMS

MEMORIES

LETTERS

A B C D E F G

H I J K L M N

O P Q R S T

U V W X Y Z

NUMBERS

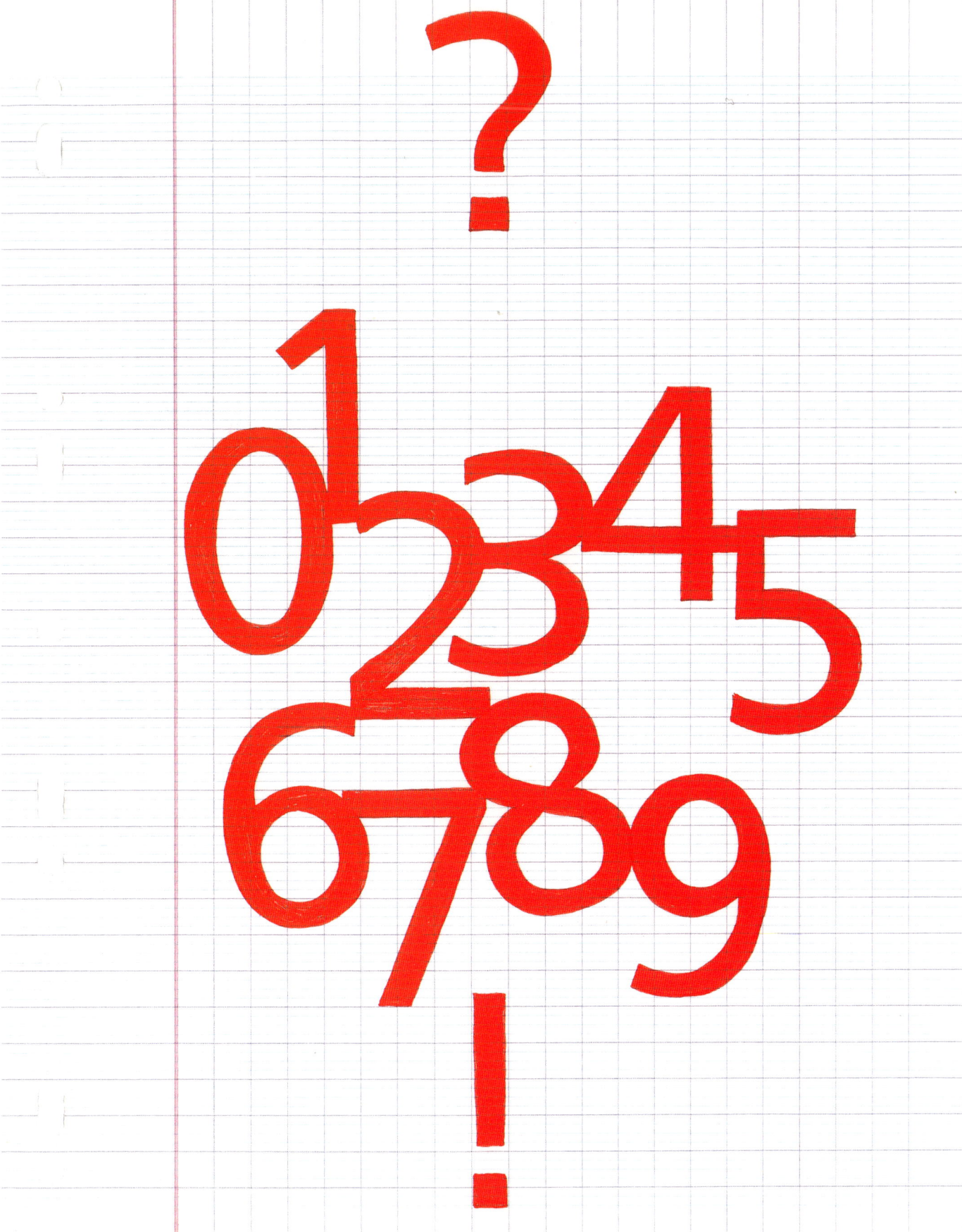

MAKE A PICTURE

WHAT'S THAT?

MAKE SOMETHING NEW

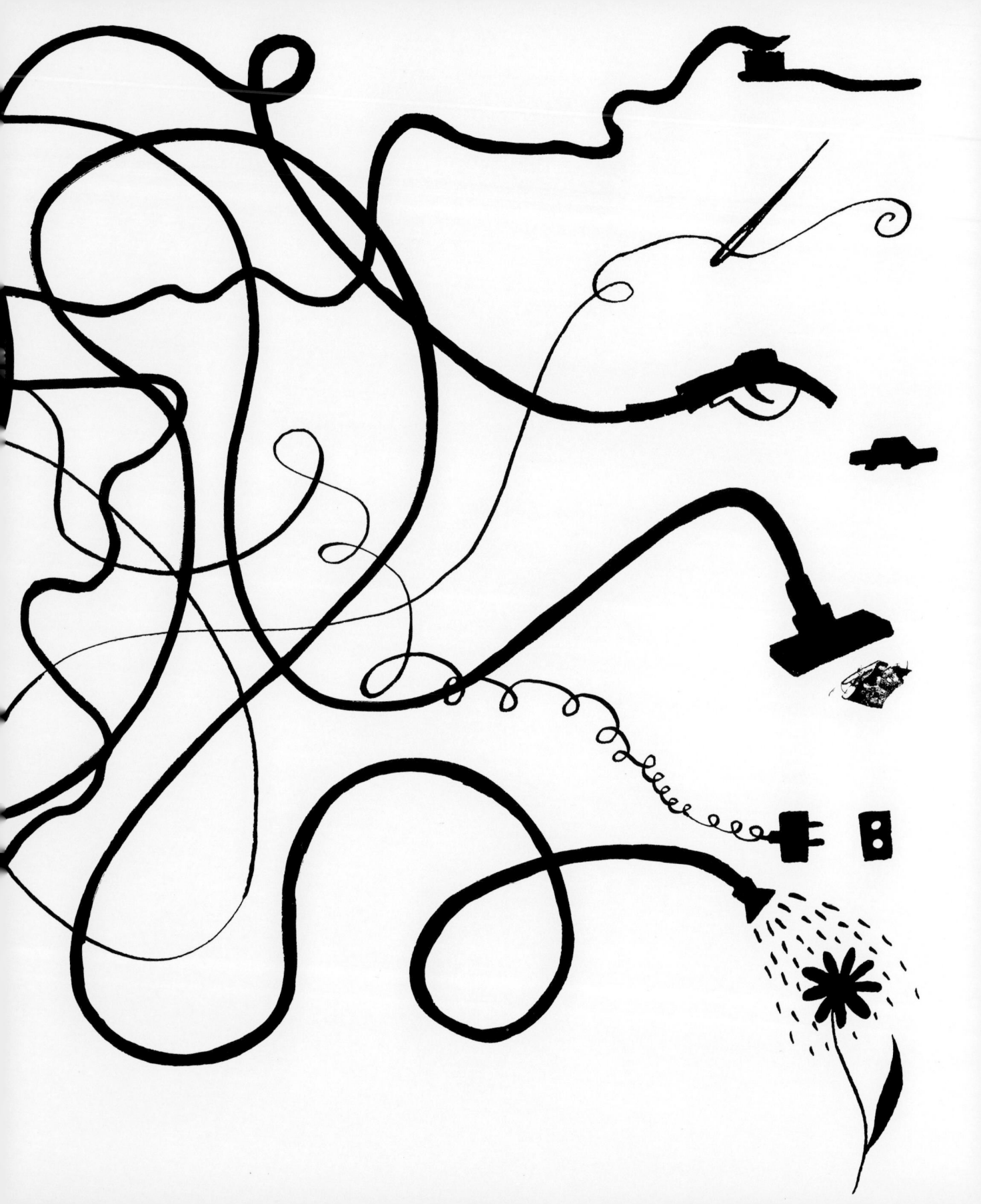

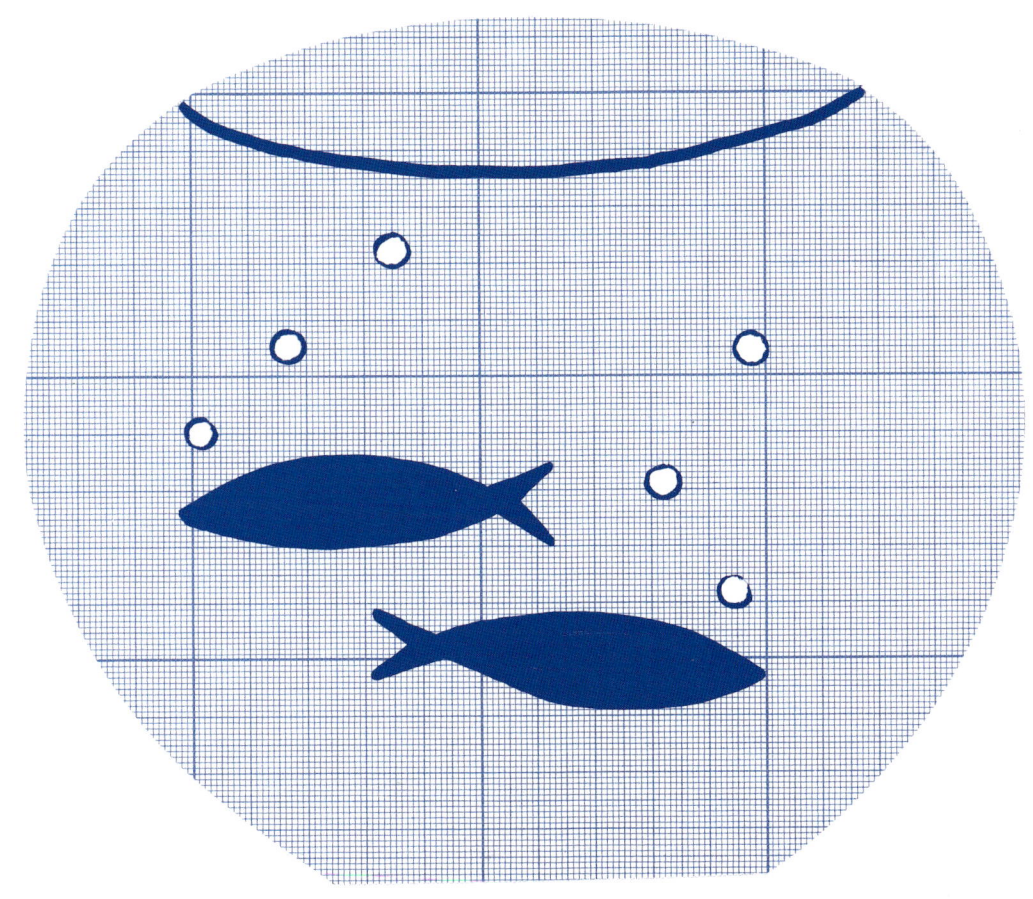

ROUND AND ROUND

IMAGINE ...

YOUR PICTURE

FIRST PUBLISHED IN ENGLISH 2005
BY TATE PUBLISHING
A DIVISION OF TATE ENTERPRISES LTD

MILLBANK, LONDON SW1P 4RG
www.tate.org.uk/publishing

ENGLISH LANGUAGE EDITION © TATE 2005
FIRST PUBLISHED IN FRENCH
UNDER THE TITLE
L'IMAGINIER
© ÉDITIONS DU SEUIL, 2005

BRITISH LIBRARY CATALOGUING
IN PUBLICATION DATA
A CATALOGUE RECORD FOR THIS BOOK
IS AVAILABLE FROM THE BRITISH LIBRARY

ISBN 1 85437 656 X

DISTRIBUTED IN THE UNITED STATES
AND CANADA BY HARRY N. ABRAMS, INC,
NEW YORK

LIBRARY OF CONGRESS CATALOGING
IN PUBLICATION DATA.

A CATALOG RECORD FOR THIS BOOK
HAS BEEN APPLIED FOR.

herve-tullet.com